Louis...

Maddie's Goal

Illustrations by
Marie-Louise Gay

Translated by
Sarah Cummins

DISCARDED

Formac Publishing Limited
Halifax, Nova Scotia
1992

Originally published as Sophie lance et compte

Copyright © 1991 la courte échelle

Translation copyright © 1992 by Formac Publishing Limited

Canadian Cataloguing in Publication Data

Leblanc, Louise, 1942-

   [Sophie lance et compte. English]

   Maddie in goal

   (First novel series)

   Translation of: Sophie lance et compte.
   ISBN 0-88780-202-8 (pbk.)
   ISBN 0-88780-203-6 (bound)

I. Gay, Marie-Louise. II Title. III Title: Sophie lance et compte. English IV. Series

PS8573.E25S6613 1992 jC843' .54 C92-098550-0
PZ7.L42Ma 1992

Formac Publishing Limited
5502 Atlantic Street
Halifax, N.S. B3H 1G4

Printed and bound in Canada

Table of contents

1
It's not funny!

It's Christmas evening, and I'm sitting alone in my room while the others are having fun. And do you know why?

Because everyone in the whole family laughed at me and I didn't think it was a bit funny. It was horrible. It made me feel as soft and squishy as a banana peel.

It started out as a very nice Christmas.

For once, I did not get a doll. And Christmas dinner was good. It was yummy!

"It is DELICIOUS," said my father. He's obsessed with proper, precise language.

Finally it was time for dessert. There was an enormous chocolate Yule log decorated with little maple sugar toadstools and Mars upon leaves.

"No, not Mars upon," my dad corrected us. "This is marzipan, MAR-ZI-PAN."

Aunt Hortense thought it would be a good time to ask us how we like school and what we want to be when we grow up.

My brother Julian, who is five years old, said that he wants to be a window washer. That's because he always has spots on his glasses.

Alexander said he wants to be a teacher. That's probably because he's so bossy. He's only seven but he's always telling me what to do.

I didn't say anything because I was busy waiting for my piece of cake. But Aunt Hortense insisted, "What about you, little Maddie? Have you decided what you want to be when you grow up?"

Do you know what I answered?

"First of all, Aunt Hortense, I am not little. I am nine years old. And when I grow up, I will be either prime minister or a writer. Or else a goaltender on a hockey team."

That was when they all burst

out laughing. All SIXTEEN of them.

The only one who didn't laugh was Gran. She understands me.

My little two-year-old sister, Angelbaby Sugarkins, didn't laugh either. That's because she didn't know what was going on, and she got scared and started to cry.

I didn't cry, although I felt like it. I went upstairs to my room.

2
Gran's advice

The worst of it is that I didn't get any chocolate Yule log. But no way am I going back down there.

"Knock-knock, Maddie!"

Oh no! Not Aunt Hortense! It's all her fault anyway.

PHEW! It's not her, it's Gran bringing me a big piece of cake. I told you she understands me.

"Come on, eat up, sweetie. We can talk afterwards."

I always do what my Gran tells me.

When I had swallowed the last crumb of that DELICIOUS Yule log, Gran said: "Do you really want to be a goaltender?"

"Well...maybe. I love hockey. And whenever Alexander and his friends ask me to play, it's because they need a goalie."

"Yes, but hockey is mostly for boys."

"I don't see why!"

"Well, Maddie, you must know that boys and girls are different."

"Of course I do, Gran! Julian is always walking around bare-bum. I know all about boys and girls. And love and babies and all."

"Really? Can you explain it

to me?"

To make sure Gran would understand it all, I lent her my book that tells how babies are made. It's a beautiful book, very interesting, with lots of pictures that show the differences between mums and dads.

"See, Gran, the differences are important when it comes to making babies. But not for playing hockey!"

"You're right, Maddie. And if being a goaltender is what you really want to do, you can do it. But it won't be easy."

"I know. They all make fun of me."

"You shouldn't worry about that. They'll stop laughing after they see your magic trick."

"What magic trick, Gran?"

"To make your dream come true, you have to bring it to life, just like a magician pulling a rabbit from a hat. When the others see that magic trick, they'll stop laughing. They will

14

look at you with eyes filled with admiration."

Gran hugged me, and then she went back downstairs with the others. While they were all having fun, I started to plan my magic trick.

3
Training

To become a goaltender, you need a good plan. I have a very good SCIENTIFIC plan.

First, I must train.

I intend to practise more often with Alexander and his buddies. This is not the ideal arrangement, but they do play hockey almost every day on the frozen pond in the neighbourhood park.

Next, I need a complete set of

goaltender gear.

That's simple. When I need it, I'll use Alexander's equipment.

Then, I need to play a real hockey game in an arena packed with fans.

I've decided to play goal for the Leprechauns. That's Alexander's team. After the Christmas holidays, they have a match with the Black Spiders, an absolutely awesome team.

I had better start my training right away.

When I get to the pond, Alexander and his buddies start laughing at me, their mouths agape like the holes in a rock singer's jeans.

I feel myself turning into a banana peel again. When you get that soft and squishy, you usually fall. Which is exactly what I do as soon as I step onto the ice.

BOOM!

Well, naturally, the pond is ringing with laughter. Sharp, mocking laughter that pierces me like poisoned darts.

I can feel my courage start to trickle away.

They'll stop laughing when they see your magic trick.

I can hear Gran's voice. Can you believe it? It's as if her words have given me wings. I feel like I have springs in my legs.

Bounding to my feet, I plant myself in front of the boys and declare, "I've come to train."

They all stop short, frozen with astonishment. Silence falls, like when the teacher comes into a

noisy classroom.

That's what gives me the inspiration to talk like a teacher.

"Come on now! What we need is a bit of discipline!"

It works! Everyone starts playing.

We play for two hours. And I think I'm beginning to get better at hockey.

Still, I've got a long way to go. The Black Spiders are supposed to be a really awesome team.

4
The puzzle

It's working! I'm in tip-top shape. I've been training every day for two weeks. The most important hockey game in my life is coming up tomorrow morning, so I've decided to take a bit of rest.

Also, I have to try on Alexander's goalie equipment while he's playing with his friends. I haven't yet told him that I'll be replacing him in the net for the Leprechauns.

I was hoping Alexander would fall sick. You'd think he would, with the cold weather we've been having. My luck must be lousy because Alexander is in the best of health.

If he doesn't catch a cold or the mumps or the measles by tonight, I'm going to have to come up with another idea.

For now, I head down to the basement, open the big duffle bag, and take out all the pieces of Alexander's hockey equipment.

PEE YOO! This stuff stinks. And there are a lot more pieces than I expected. The best way to figure this all out is to put it together like a puzzle, on the couch.

I start with the easiest parts—
the helmet, the mask, and a bit
lower down, the leg pads.

The rest is simple. It's all got to
go in between.

Still, after I'm finished, there's
one little piece that I can't fit in.
A strange little piece.

YIPES! I hear a noise. Quick,
I hide behind the couch.

PHEW! It's only Julian. But
when he sees the goaltender
puzzle, he starts to howl: "Mum!
A ghost! There's a ghost sitting
on the couch! Mummy!"

Of course, Mum comes run-
ning.

"Julian, really! It's not a ghost,
it's only Alexander's goalie out-
fit. You know he always leaves
his things lying around."

She's right. So do you know

what she goes and does?

She takes my puzzle apart, and puts all the pieces away in the hockey bag. GRRR!

I had to hold my breath the whole time and stifle a little cry of triumph because I figured out where the funny little piece goes. It's a dickie-protector. Hee! hee! hee!

Well, now I've got it all figured out, but it's too late to try on the goalie outfit.

Too bad. I'll have to try it on just before the game. It's bound to fit just fine.

The important thing is knowing where all the pieces of the puzzle go.

5
Alexander's dream comes true

"ACHOOO!"

Alexander is in my room and he's just sneezed. I seize my chance.

"Alexander, you poor thing, you must be coming down with a cold!"

"I am not!"

"You are, you're getting sick."

"Baloney! I should know whether I'm sick or not. You're

acting weird. You invited me to your room and all. That doesn't happen very often."

Alexander is such a grump. I think he suspects that I'm up to something.

Fortunately, I am as wily as a fox…or is it a coyote? So I just pretend to go along with him.

"You're right, I am acting weird. I've decided to give you most of my things."

"What!?!"

"I'm cleaning up. You can take whatever you want."

"WHAT!?! You're crazy! I don't believe you."

"Stop saying WHAT and just take what you want. You'll see if I'm kidding."

"Wow! Okay, I want your yellow bear…and your caterpillar with yellow spots…and your monster with yellow paws."

"Is that all?"

"NO! That's only the stuffed animals. I also want your transformers…your piggy-bank with the lock…your yellow knee-socks…your space marbles, and your Ice Machine tape."

"WHOA!"

"Oh yes, I also want your book that shows how to make babies."

"No way! You can't have that. Anyway, I've lent it to Gran. Okay, let's move all this stuff into your room."

Alexander doesn't protest. This is the first time he's ever done what I told him to do. He's probably afraid I'll change my mind.

When he's done putting my

things in with his, I continue with my wily plan.

"I hope you're happy now?"

"Yeah, this is like a dream," says Alexander.

"You know, I have dream too."

"What's your dream?"

"To play goalie for the Leprechauns tomorrow."

"WHAT!?!"

"So let's trade. Your dream for my dream. It's simple. I'll let you have my stuff, and you let me play goalie instead of you."

Alexander is silent. I don't want to let him think about it for too long.

"Well?"

"Well, I'm a bit suspicious. And anyway, it's impossible."

"Nothing's impossible, when you dream. Gran told me so. The

first thing is for you to get sick."

"What do you mean, get sick?"

"You know, get sick, like when you don't feel like going to school."

Now we're talking! Alexander and I start to giggle, then we laugh our heads off.

It's great to have a laugh with someone!

6
Family conference

"ACHOOO! Hee-hee-hee! ACHOOO! Hee-hee-hee!"

"Will you stop laughing!"

Alexander has just fallen sick and he's having the time of his life.

That's the trouble with little kids, they never know when to stop. They can never be serious.

And now is the time to get serious.

We have to convince my father that Alexander is too sick to play hockey tomorrow, and that a replacement must be found for him right away.

My mother and Angelbaby are taking a bath. My dad and Julian are piling wood in the fireplace to make a fire.

In the script I've prepared, Alexander has the leading role. He has to say exactly what I've told him to say.

"Dad—ACHOOO! I have a sore throat, my tummy hurts, my nose itches, and I have a headache."

"Is that all?" asks my dad.

I can't believe it! My father is heartless! I know I shouldn't interfere, but under the circumstances it seems necessary.

"Alexander is VERY sick, Dad. I don't think he should play hockey tomorrow."

"What? The game with the Black Spiders? I would be very surprised if Alexander were to miss that. Let's wait till tomorrow to decide. He might be feeling better."

I answer firmly, "No, tomorrow it will be too late to find

someone to take his place."

My father is even more surprised. "What about that little Flaherty kid?"

"The little Flaherty kid cannot do it. He's a defenseman. The Black Spiders will eat the Leprechauns alive if we don't have a REAL goalie who knows how to play."

"And where, pray tell, would they find such a marvel?" my father inquires as he lights a match to start the fire.

I take a deep breath and answer in a rush: "Right-here-in-our-living-room-the-marvel-is-me."

My father is so astonished he drops his match, which falls onto the rug and starts to smoulder and smoke and stink.

Julian pulls off his glasses and

runs from the room, screaming, "FIRE! FIRE!"

He rushes back in with my mother and Angelbaby. They're wrapped up in a huge towel, their hair dripping lather all over their faces. My mother seems upset.

"What's going on in here?"

I nudge Alexander with my elbow. He pipes up, "I'm going to be sick tomorrow, so Maddie has to take my place. Even though she's not as good as me, she's still better than the Flaherty kid. That's all."

My mother turns on her heel and walks out of the room, looking even more upset. Angelbaby is wailing because she has soap in her eyes.

My dad keeps repeating, "Ah,

I understand…I understand now…"

Alexander and I wait. And wait.

After an eternity my father says, "We'll have to convince the coach that this is a good idea."

FANTASTIC! I'm sure we'll have no trouble convincing the coach.

Do you know why? Because the coach of the Leprechauns is Uncle Anthony!

7
Maddie in the net

My father managed to convince Uncle Anthony. But Uncle Anthony has not managed to convince the Leprechauns, that's for sure.

They're huddled in one corner of the locker room looking over at me and whispering.

You know what I feel like? A white chocolate in a box of dark chocolates. A visible-minority chocolate, as my father would say.

Gran was right. Becoming a goaltender is a very ambitious dream for a girl to make come true.

The siren announces the beginning of the game.

The Leprechauns are out of the locker room in a flash. The best my uncle can come up with as I follow them is, "It's too late to turn back now."

Great. A real pep talk.

I feel like a poor abandoned visible-minority chocolate about to melt under all this goalie equipment.

Then do I get a shock! I catch a glimpse of myself in the mirror. I look totally ridiculous.

Alexander's goalie pads are

too short for me. With my two legs sticking out below and ending in my neon yellow skates, I look exactly like a duck.

I look hideous.

Think of the admiring looks when the magician finally pulls the rabbit out of the hat.

Gran! I can hear Gran again! And again, her words seem to give me wings, just like the other day at the park.

I go out of the locker room. The murmur of the crowd reaches my ears. It's like a magnet pulling me in.

I enter the arena. The first three rows of seats are packed. I jump onto the ice, as light as a feather. I glide, I float to my goal, under the bright lights.

The referee's whistle calls for

silence. Then, all at once the magic seems to drain away with the crowd's noise.

I start to shake. My goalie out-fit seems heavier and heavier and I'm getting softer and squishier.

For the first time in my life, I've got rink fright! It's TERRIFYING!

The Black Spiders are going to eat me alive. I know it.

8
She shoots, she scores!

The third period has just begun. Right now the play is down at the other end, and I have time to tell you how the game has gone.

Despite a rocky start, I was magnificent for twenty minutes. I blocked every shot—three incredible saves. The first period ended with no score.

The second period was slightly different. No one played well.

When we headed back to the locker room, the Black Spiders were leading 8 to 7.

Of course, the Leprechauns all said that it was my fault, and— YI YI YIKES! Watch out! They're coming back down here. Everyone's in front of the net and I can't see a thing.

WHERE IS THE PUCK?

PHEW! It's behind the goal. No, there it is, it's…in the net. I don't believe it.

9 to 7.

I have to concentrate, that's for certain.

The little Flaherty kid passes the puck to the big Figuereido kid, the best player on the Leprechauns. He breaks away down to the opposing goal, dekes the goaltender, and scores! 9 to 8.

Face off. Play slows down, but time seems to be speeding up. It looks like it's all over for the Leprechauns.

The Spiders seem to get a fresh spurt of energy. Number 7 passes to Number 15, who passes back to Number 7, who flips the puck to Number 22.

Number 22 is the biggest Spider. He is a MONSTER, skating right at me, with the other players trailing behind.

I am the only Leprechaun in front of him. If I'm going to stop him, I'll have to come out of the net.

So I do, squeezing my eyes shut.

BANG!

I've just been flattened by that MONSTER. I see stars, big

spidery stars.

The crowd howls.

Julian yells, "You flunking bannister!"

Another voice calls out, "Brute!"

Gran cries, "You leave my little sweetie alone!"

My father shouts urgently, "Go on! SHOOT!"

"What do you mean, shoot?" I answer.

I look around.

Spider Number 22 has crashed into the boards. Other Spiders are dropping like flies. All of the Leprechauns are behind me.

I spot the puck at my feet. For a split second, I think of all the admiring looks.

Now is the time to perform my

magic trick and pull the rabbit out of my hat.

I get to my feet. The other goalie has left his net, certain that the Spiders have already won the game. There are only a few metres between us. And only a few seconds left to play.

Then everything seems to happen in slow motion, like in the replays on TV.

I shoot...the puck passes between the goalie's legs...it slithers...it slides...

SCORE!!!

There is an explosion of joy from the crowd. The Leprechauns come skating towards me, tossing their gloves in the air and yelling.

HOORAY! YIPPEE!!! The Black Spiders didn't beat us!

YIPPEE!   HOORAY   FOR MADDIE!

I don't even have time to see their admiring looks because they all pile on top of me and pound my back.

IT'S WONDERFUL!

9
A cold shower

What a feeling! I can't get over it. It is really an UNFOR-GETTABLE experience to make your dream come true.

When I get back home, I am completely exhausted. I let Julian, Gran, and my dad tell everyone about my amazing feat.

It is just as exciting to hear it told as it was to live it. While I listen, I devour the delicious pizza that my mother has made.

"It is really very unusual for a goalie to score," my dad points out.

Julian tells everyone that he insulted the monster Spider when he yelled "You flunking bannister" at him. Gran bubbles with laughter and Angelbaby claps her hands. Everyone is happy.

Except Alexander.

He is such a stinker. Not the tiniest word of congratulations. He won't talk to me all afternoon.

I decide to make the first move and I go up to his room. Besides, I want to borrow the Ice Machine tape. I feel like listening to some music.

But all Alexander will say is, "No. This is MY tape."

And, "MUM!"

Naturally, my mum comes running. And do you know what she tells me?

"Alexander got sick, he couldn't play hockey, and he had to stay home. So this Ice Machine cassette is his. And these are HIS things. Do you understand?"

WHEW! What a cold shower!

The next time I decide to make my dream come true, I'm going to think it over. It is wonderful when it happens, but it is very difficult because of what you have to give up along the way, that's for sure.

The First Novel series

If you enjoyed this book, you'll enjoy these other First Novels — available now at your local bookstore!

Arthur's Dad

by Ginette Anfousse

Arthur's dad is about to give up because he can't find a babysitter for Arthur. He has already had twenty-three! But now perhaps Arthur has met his match ...

That's Enough, Maddie

by Louise Leblanc

Maddie has quite a problem. Her whole family is getting on her nerves. So she decides to run away from home ... but what do you do when supper time rolls around?

The Swank Prank

by Bertrand Gauthier

Hank and Frank Swank are twins. Trying to be the smartest kids in school takes a lot of work. Can they do it?

Swank Talk

by Bertrand Gauthier

The Swank twins have found a way to confuse everyone: no one can understand what they're saying! It takes another set of twins to put them back in touch with the world.

Mooch and Me

by Gilles Gauthier

Carl and his best friend Mooch are nine. But, Mooch is a dog and that makes him 63! He is old, deaf and almost blind, and he gets Carl into lots of trouble. But Carl thinks he's the best dog that ever lived!

Hang on, Mooch

by Gilles Gauthier

Mooch is in the dog pound. And when Carl finally gets her released, it looks like her days are numbered ...

The Loonies Arrive

by Christiane Duchesne

One night Christopher finds some little people under his pillow — no more than three centimetres tall! It's not easy learning how to look after a collection of little people who make their home in your room ...

DISCARDED